For:

_____

From:

_____

Christmas
Cheer
for The Grouchy Ladybug

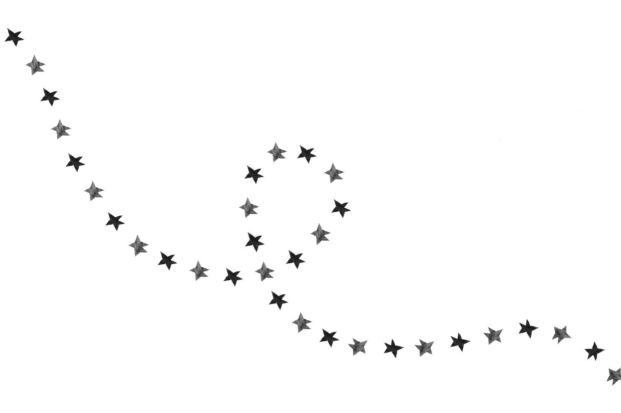

ISBN 978-0-06-293226-6

Book design by Rachel Zegar

19   20   21   22   23   SCP   10   9   8   7   6   5   4   3   2   1

❖

First Edition

Christmas Cheer

for The Grouchy Ladybug

By Eric Carle

HARPER
An Imprint of HarperCollinsPublishers

Christmas

means

JOY

for all.

Snowflakes

glisten

white,

and
fires
burn
bright...

. . . time to have a
ball.

Bells **ring,**

and everyone **sings...**

. . . no matter how

BIG

or

small.

Presents
wait under the
tree,

and you just might see . . .

...**stockings**

hung on the wall.

Shhh, do you hear?

Why, it's . . .

all our
friends
spreading
holiday cheer!

Christmas

brings out the very best . . .

. . . even in those
grouchier
than the rest.

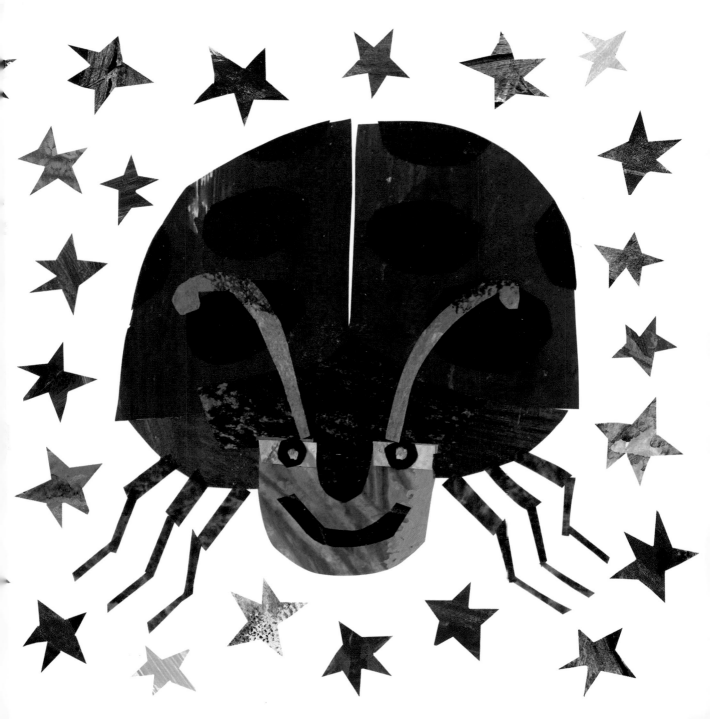

MERRY CH

RISTMAS!

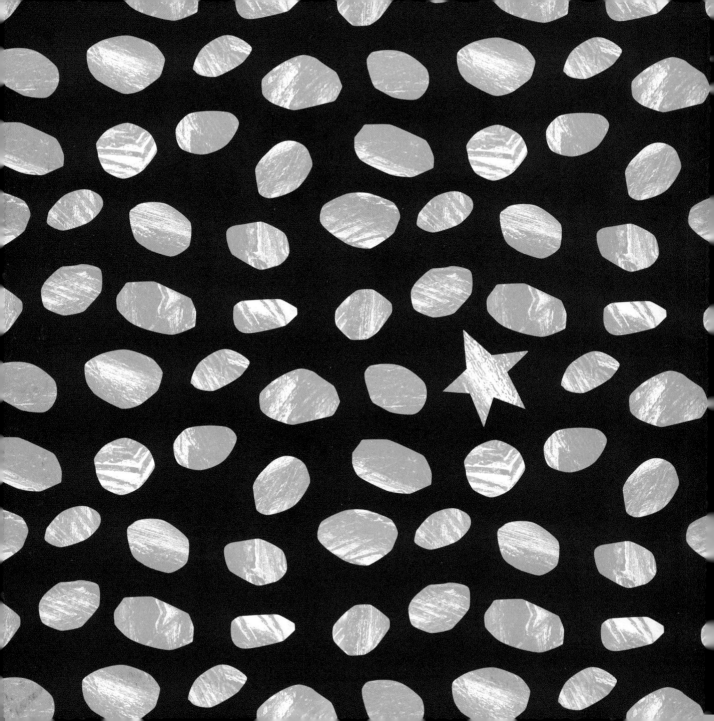